Northern Narratives #3

TALL TALES OF ALASKA

SITKA AK

Where Cultures, Customs & Countries Collided

W.R. Kozey

ISBN 978-1-954896-47-5 paperback
ISBN 978-1-954896-46-8 ebook

Printed in United States

Illustrations and cover design: Sam Grubitz
Cover image: Todd—stock.adobe.com

Southeast Alaska map iStock.com/Artist Rainer Lesniewski.

Limit of Liability: No representations are made with respect to the accuracy or completeness of the contents of this work and the author specifically states that all the stories in this collection are works of fiction. This work is published and sold with the understanding that neither the publisher nor the author are historians. For factual information about Sitka, Alaska, a professional historian should be sought. Neither the publisher nor the author shall be liable for damages arising from the reading of this book.

Fathom Publishing Company
PO Box 200448 | Anchorage, AK 99520
Fathom Publishing.com

To my mother, who gives endlessly
and never asks for anything in return.
Your love has always been my greatest
strength and it has carried me through
more than you'll ever know.

Contents

Acknowledgments

I would like to begin by acknowledging the Indigenous peoples of Alaska and their ancestral homelands. I want to pay my respects to all the Tribes that call this land their home and recognize the deep and abiding connections they have to this place.

I would also like to acknowledge the brave and tenacious souls who traveled to Alaska seeking fortune and adventure.
For it is their experiences and struggles that line these pages and without them there is no book.

Finally, I want to express my gratitude to all those who have contributed to this work, whether through guidance, support, or inspiration. This collection would not have been possible without their contributions— thank you.

Where did Sitka get its name?

To know a place is to not just know its people, its streets and shops, or its landscape. No, it is more than that. You need to know its history, and its name gives you a glimpse into that past.

And the name "Sitka" carries with it a colorful story full of fierce battles, timeworn traditions, and the combining of cultures that have shaped this community, and the people that call it home. From the Tlingit's deep-rooted connection to the tides to the Russian ambitions that brought them to the Americas, Sitka's name is etched into each wave and every mountain you see in town.

So to start, we need to go back, long before the arrival of Russian explorers and settlers, to a time when the land we now know as Sitka was home to only the Indigenous peoples, the Tlingit. The Tlingit have a deep connection to the land and sea, which is reflected in their language and the names they give the places they live. Hence, the original Tlingit name for Sitka was Shee At'iká—or Sheet'ká, for short—meaning "people of the tide." It was a name that signified not only the Tlingit people's intimate connection with the ocean's rhythms—the tides that brought sustenance and life to their shores—but also their profound understanding of their environment.

For centuries, the Tlingit thrived along the rugged coastline. And the name Sheet'ká became more than just a geographical designation; it reflected their identity, culture, and way of life. It spoke of a society aligned with the cycles of nature, fishing the abundant waters, hunting in the dense forests, and passing down stories that connected each generation to the tides and the land.

But, as we all know, the Tlingit people eventually had some company. And the arrival of the Russian explorers in the late 18th century would mark a significant turning point in the region's history—a turning point which would see rising tensions, battles fought, and names changed. This was due to the Russians quickly recognizing the strategic and economic importance of the location and their decision to build a settlement there.

Now, I won't go into detail over the wars won and lost right now, there is more of that in the stories to come, but in the end, the Russians would win a decisive battle which would allow them to build a fortified outpost—an outpost they named Novo-Arkhangelsk or New Archangel. And from that moment on, the settlement became a symbol of Russian expansion and ambition, and the location became their center of trade and governance in North America.

For a time, New Archangel was the place where Russia's determination and desire to transplant their culture and authority in this distant land, much like how the other European colonial powers did, took place. A desire which resulted in new foods, customs, and architecture arriving on Sitka's shores.

However, despite the Russian presence in town, the Tlingit people remained deeply connected to their ancestral lands, and the name "Sheet'ká" persisted in the hearts and minds of the Indigenous population. And in 1867, when the United States purchased Alaska from Russia, this connection and this name would once again be honored.

That's right, the transfer of power brought about many changes. For one, American soldiers replaced the Russian ones; English replaced Russian as the language used in town; and fur traders quickly became prospectors eager to turn Alaska into the next great goldrush.

Of course, all of these significant shifts play parts in the tales to come, but for this story, the most notable transition was one which saw the name of the town officially become Sitka—the anglicized version of Sheet'ká—the blending of both the Indigenous heritage of the area and the new American administration.

It isn't just in the name, though. Sitka, as it is known today, is a place where you can literally see the confluence of cultures that occurred in this area. It is in the historic Russian buildings that line its streets, the Tlingit totem poles that populate its parks, and the star-spangled flags that wave in the wind.

So, to bring this full-circle, to know a place is to know its name, and the name Sitka embodies this little Alaskan town's enormous historical significance. It does so by carrying with it the echoes of Shee At'iká and the resilience of the Tlingit people, the ambitions of the Russian settlers, and the aspirations of the American pioneers. It is a name that speaks to the people that call this town home, but also to the layered history of Alaska, a place that has had to continually learn to adapt, endure, and evolve.

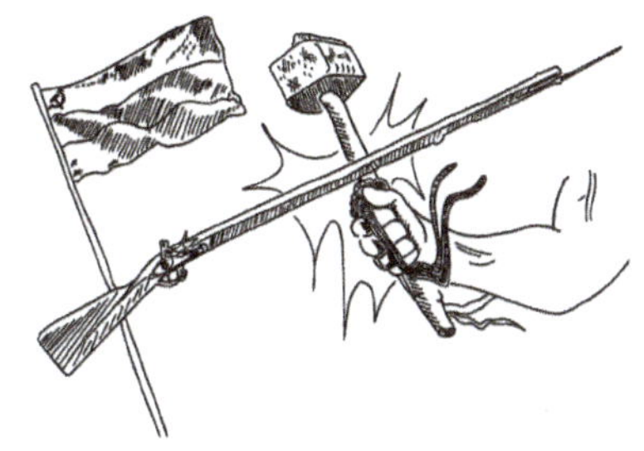

How did Russia
come to occupy Sitka?

Now that we know a little bit more
about Sitka and its origins, it is time
that we take a chapter out of history and
look at how Sitka came to be occupied
by Russia. And to do so, we need to
recognize that, in the early 1800s, the
shores of Southeast Alaska were seen as
more than just a landscape of towering
trees and mountains—they were the
frontline of a fierce struggle between the
Tlingit people and Russian invaders.

But before we get to the defining moment in 1804, the Battle of Sitka, we need to go back even further to 1802 and Russia's first settlement in the area.

In the early days of Russian expansion, Russian explorers established their first settlement in Sitka Sound in what is now called Old Sitka. And for a time, the Russians lived in relative peace with the Tlingit people. Both respected one another's space with neither side looking to encroach on the other's land or resources. However, that all ended when Russia had the bright idea to build a barracks—a structure that meant more than the Russians had decided to stay. It meant soldiers, it meant an army, and it meant that they were planning an invasion.

So, what did the Tlingit do? They laid siege on Old Sitka, slaying all of the Russians there and burning every building, including the would-be barracks. The attack was a message, one that was heard loud and clear in St. Petersburg, the Russian capital at the time. A message that said "Alaska is more than just land to us, it is our heritage, our culture, our way of life, and we will defend it."

The Tlingit were not only fierce warriors but also masterful strategists. And in anticipation of the Russian return, they fortified a position known as Shís'gi Noow on what is called Castle Hill today. Here, they constructed a strong defensive fort, Noow Tlein, with ingenious engineering designed to withstand a Russian assault.

Fast forward to October 1804. The Russians returned with battleships laden with cannons seeking vengeance for their fallen comrades. But despite their superior firepower, the Tlinget still had an advantage. Not only was their fort fortified to repel cannon fire, the Russian troops harbored a deep-seated fear of the Tlingit.

Back in Russia, stories had circulated about Tlingit warriors clad in yellow cedar armor rising up as if from the dead after being shot and charging with relentless ferocity. These tales, steeped in both truth and myth, only heightened the dread among the Russian forces.

The siege began with a bombardment of cannon fire, thundering as cannon balls pounded the Tlingit fort. Yet, the angled walls did their job, deflecting the cannonballs and preserving the fort's integrity. Inside, the Tlingit warriors held their ground undaunted by the relentless assault.

The battle raged for days, each side fighting with a determination born of survival and sovereignty. For the Tlingit, every moment was a stand against erasure. For the Russians, every advance was met with a fortitude that tested their resolve.

In the end, the conflict came down to ammunition, the one thing in short supply for the Tlingit. And eventually, despite their resilience, they made the difficult decision to retreat.

Under the cover of darkness, they slipped away, moving to a more secure location inland. A move which many have falsely assumed was a surrender, but in reality, was a calculated choice to preserve their people and continue their resistance.

Regardless of how it was viewed though, the Russians were now in control of the battlefield. They established a settlement on the ruins of Noow Tlein and called it, as we learned earlier, New Archangel—a town that would grow with Russian expansion and eventually be called Sitka.

Today, the site of the Battle of Sitka is part of the Sitka National Historic Park, more commonly known by the locals as Totem Park. It is a place where you can walk the hallowed ground, see the totem poles and serene beauty, and learn about this historic conflict.

And whether you were aware of the Battle of 1804 before this story or not, at least now you know a little bit more about the nuances that led to the Russian occupation of Alaska. You've learned about the yellow cedar armor, you've been impressed by the angled fort walls built to repel cannon fire, and you can better appreciate the Tlingit's strategic retreat. For the Battle's legacy is not just a memory but a living reminder of the Tlingit's resilient spirit—a spirit that continues to inspire and resonate with those that call Sitka home.

Where did the Tlingit go after the Battle of 1804?

As we learned from the previous story, the Tlingit did not lose against the Russians, nor did they surrender, but what they did do still bewilders folks generations later.

Following the fierce clash at the Battle of Sitka in 1804, they vanished— disappearing into the dense rainforest and uncharted wilderness, a hidden world known only to them. The story of their retreat is one of tactical brilliance, ancestral wisdom, and their people's profound connection to the land. For it allowed them to defy the odds and shape the legend of a people who refused to be conquered.

To recap, in the aftermath of the fierce bombardment and unyielding assault by the Russian forces, the Tlingit faced a dire situation. Their fort at Castle Hill was indefensible. Supplies were dwindling and fear was growing, but surrender was never an option. So, in the middle of the night, the entire community retreated to a place so remote, so hidden, that even today, it remains shrouded in mystery.

From what I've been told by locals, this sanctuary, deep within what is now known as Baranof Island, is a place untouched by time and inaccessible to outsiders. Only the Tlingit's innate understanding of the land allowed them to navigate the secret paths and hidden passages of this treacherous terrain. They moved silently, leaving no trace, to this hidden refuge where they could regroup and plan their next move.

For the Tlingit, this sanctuary was more than a physical refuge; it was a spiritual stronghold, a place where they could maintain their cultural practices, honor their ancestors, and prepare for the ongoing struggle with the Russians. It was here that they not only survived but thrived by launching precise raids that left the Russians constantly looking over their shoulders, haunted by the thought of their enemy appearing from nowhere to attack from some unreachable sanctuary.

One particularly chilling tale speaks of Tlingit warriors, clad in their near-impenetrable yellow cedar armor, emerging from the mists at dawn, striking swiftly and sinking some of the larger Russian ships in port, and then disappearing back into the shadows. To the Russians, it was these attacks that left them feeling as if the island itself was conspiring against them, masking the Tlingit's movements and shielding them from their enemies.

These feelings continued all throughout the Russian occupation of Alaska, with the Tlingit remaining a constant and formidable presence— one which their strategic retreat only strengthened. Not only did it showcase their warrior prowess, it highlighted their relationship to their ancestral lands. And because of this, the Russians made every effort to coexist peacefully moving forward, often abiding by Tlingit law and respecting their autonomy.

As for their hidden refuge today, it is still a mystery, a powerful symbol of the Tlingit's resilience, their unyielding spirit, and a lasting statement of Tlingit sovereignty.

Why did Russia choose Sitka for their capital?

When Russian explorers first set their sights on the rugged shores of Sitka, they saw more than just wilderness, they saw opportunity. But before we get into why Sika, we need to first look at why Alaska. And to do that, we need to go all the way back to the 1700s.

For some time, Russia sat on the sidelines, watching other nations expand their empires. However, in the mid-1700s, the Russian Tsar felt it was time to join the party. So, he petitioned a ship to travel east and explore the new world. The captain of that ship, Vitus Bering.

Now, despite the Bering Strait being named after her captain, this ship's journey was far from smooth sailing. From what I've been told, during their maiden voyage, Bering and his crew ran into some trouble just off of the Alaskan coast. Some say there was a disagreement amongst the crew. Others say the ship experienced some issues after hitting some ice. Either way though, they were forced to seek safe harbor along the mainland to regroup.

While on land, the crew quickly worked their way through the ship's provisions and needed to find another source of food to sustain themselves. What they found were sea otters, and lots of them. Now, this is important for two reasons. First, the sea otters provided the sustenance the Russians needed to survive in the Alaskan climate while they fixed their boat. And second, sea otter pelts were highly prized back in Russia, and the discovery of them would surely earn the group praise upon their return.

And it surely did. After all, the Bering Strait isn't named the Bering Strait for no reason. That said, their discovery did more than just put their names on the map, it sparked a massive movement in Russia leading to multiple merchant ships traveling to Alaska in search of sea otters.

This went on for quite some time, with independently-funded ships traveling the distance to Alaska in hopes to strike it rich. That is, until the Russian Tsar decided that the sea otter trade in Alaska would be better run by the state.

Now, the reasoning for moving away from free enterprise isn't fully known. Some say that the Alaskan sea otter trade had garnered too much attention from other nations, and Russia's role in the area needed further solidification. Others say this decision was based on greed because the Tsar didn't feel like he was getting a big enough piece of the pie. Either way, the Russian-American Company was born, and the search for a home for this company began.

Of course, Sika Sound's large sea otter population made it appealing. And its abundant food sources could sustain settlers and allow for the town to grow. Not to mention, the town's topography offered unparalleled advantages against attack. Castle Hill, where Russia chose to build its administrative and military headquarters, provided a commanding view of the surrounding waters.

However, the most compelling reasons for Sitka's selection as the capital were rooted in commerce and economics. Positioned at the midpoint of Russian America, Sitka was ideally located between the Aleutians and Northern

California, facilitating the movement of goods and resources, and making it a vital hub for trade and communication.

But as important as this was, I hope this story has shown you that there really isn't just one singular reason to choose Sitka, there are many. It is a special place situated on the furthest reaches of Alaska's Southeastern coast where, during Russian occupation, ambition and culture converged—a history that still colors this town's streets.

Ice Trade … Seriously?

So far you've read all about the burgeoning fur trade of the 1800s, of the valuable sea otter pelts Russia would trade to China for silks and spices, and how Russian settlers discovered an abundance of sea otters living in and around Sitka.

But, at this same time, another trade was blossoming—ice. That's right, sea otters weren't the only game in town. The Russian-American Company was seeking to diversify and Sitka's lakes became the unlikely source of a booming industry.

Long before modern refrigeration, ice was a luxury reserved only for those with access to nature's coldest resources. And amidst Sitka's towering mountains and dense forests, Alaskan ice—clear, pristine, and abundant—became the surprising cornerstone of the new, international ice trade.

Sitka, more specifically Swan Lake, a tranquil body of water nestled near Sitka, became the epicenter of this icy commerce. Each winter as the lake froze over, hardy men armed with saws and chisels ventured onto its surface, cutting massive blocks of virgin ice—the clearest and purest one could find. Of course, the work was grueling, and more often than not conducted in subzero temperatures, but the juice was worth the squeeze.

Once harvested, the ice was transported to Sitka's docks where it was prepared for the long and perilous journey to Gold Rush era California.

At the time, the demand for ice there was insatiable. It was used to preserve food, cool drinks, and provide a touch of luxury beneath the heat of the California sun. That is, if you could afford it. For those who had struck it rich in the goldfields, a block of ice from Alaska was not just a commodity used for practical purposes— it was a symbol of wealth and refinement.

The ice trade quickly became one of the most important assets of the Russian-American Company. Its profits helped sustain the colony and fund further ventures. However, as we all know, the winds of change were soon to blow. And in 1867, the United States purchased Alaska from Russia, a transaction that forever altered the fate of the territory.

Among the assets transferred as a part of the deal was the thriving ice trade. And soon, American entrepreneurs, eager to capitalize on this northern bounty, recognized the value of Alaskan ice and continued the enterprise with the same enthusiasm. They expanded trade routes, increased production, and even brought their own innovations to Alaska to further capitalize on this growing economy.

It is a story of the men and women who braved the cold, dark winters and saw potential when others saw only ice. The trade truly embodied the pioneering spirit of Alaska, a place where the land itself is both an obstacle and an asset.

Today though, when looking out over the calm waters of Swan Lake, it is easy to forget the lake's industrious history, one that was quite literally carved from its surface. But for those who know, which now includes all of you, the story of Alaska's ice trade remains frozen in history—a shimmering chapter of Sitka's past, one that saw blocks of ice from the far north bring a touch of the Arctic to the sunny shores of California.

Why was Sitka called the Paris of the Pacific?

If you're reading this book, the odds are you've visited or are planning to visit Sitka. And if you've done either of these, you have some semblance of what the town looks like. And you know its appearance has very little in common with Paris, nor does it resemble any European city for that matter. There are no cobblestone streets, no charming cafes with outdoor seating, and there is definitely no Eiffel Tower.

But despite all that it is lacking, Sitka still maintains the moniker, the Paris of the Pacific. And if you keep on reading, you'll find out why this sleepy town on the edge of the world was once compared to the City of Light.

The story of Sitka's pseudonym begins with, you guessed it, the sea otter—that small, unassuming creature whose dense, luxurious fur became currency enough to fuel an empire. These pelts were traded like treasure, more valuable than gold in the markets of Europe and China. Just six of these little pelts were enough for a person to retire on! And in Sitka, they were in no short supply, making the city the center point for Russian commerce in the Americas.

The town grew quickly and at its heart rose St. Michael's Cathedral, its green domes and onion spires standing tall against the gray sky, a constant reminder of the European presence

on this distant shore. The Cathedral's
bronze bells could be heard all over
town, mingling with the lively clamor of
market stalls where traders haggled over
pelts, beads, and silks. The energy of the
town was palpable—a subtle blending of
the familiar and the foreign, a cultural
crossroads where Russian, Indigenous,
and international influences were all
merging in unexpected ways.

Perched on top of Castle Hill
overlooking the harbor, the Chief
Manager's house was the beating heart
of Sitka's social life. Russian officials,
military officers, and their families
would gather, dance, dine, and discuss
the delicate politics of empire. Grand
balls and soirées unfolded beneath
glittering chandeliers, the rooms alive
with the swish of silks, and the crisp
click of polished boots. The music
was European, but the backdrop was
distinctly Alaskan—a lavish performance

set against the raw, wild, and indifferent wilderness.

That wasn't all though, Sitka's streets, a maze of wooden houses, and winding alleys, became alive with the hum of everyday life. Schools and libraries sprang up bringing European thoughts and ideals to the town's residents. Craftsmen, teachers, and sailors carved out routines that blended the comforts of Europe with the rugged reality of the Alaskan coast. And the harbor never rested. Ships from America, China, and Europe were anchored side by side, their crews speaking in a jumble of languages, putting on display the trade routes that were now weaving this new township into the global network. It became a place that felt both small and vast, a crossroads of stories that stretched far beyond its shores.

Yet, as the years passed, Sitka's fortunes soon shifted. The sale of Alaska to the United States in 1867 marked the end of Russian rule, and with it, the city's brief but brilliant chapter as Alaska's gateway port to international trade ended.

The capital moved north to Juneau, the grand balls faded, and Sitka's once-bustling streets grew quieter. But the names of those streets, the architecture of the buildings, and the stories still remain, speaking of the time when it was more than just a town—it had been a daring experiment in grandeur and adaptation, where cultures collided, and the future felt as if it were being written in real-time. It was the Paris of the Pacific, a place where ambition met the frontier and, for a fleeting moment, they danced.

Is that the original
St. Michael's Cathedral?

Okay, so in the previous story you heard about the important role the Chief Manager's home atop Castle Hill and St. Michael's Cathedral played during Sitka's earlier years. However, only one of these two structures is still in existence. That's right, situated smack dab in the middle of Sitka's busiest street stands St. Michael's Cathedral, a silent witness to the town's historical trials and triumphs.

But is it the original? Before we get

to that though, it would be an injustice to this building's significance if we didn't share a little bit of its history.

St. Michael's Cathedral was completed in 1848 under the guidance of Bishop Innocent, and at the time it was a modern marvel in Alaska. The iconic green domes and graceful architecture were like nothing that had been seen before on these shores. And for over a century, the Cathedral played host to masses, baptisms, weddings, and funerals, serving as the spiritual hub for the Russian community.

But in January of 1966, tragedy struck. A fierce and unrelenting fire engulfed St. Michael's, reducing the beloved Cathedral to smoldering ruins. The community could only watch as the Cathedral burned and its steeples collapsed. It is said that the heat from the fire was so intense that the church bells trapped inside melted, sending a stream of bronze flowing down Lincoln Street like a molten river.

Now, the what is well documented. The fire, fed by winter winds, consumed everything in its path. As for the how and the why, this is less agreed upon. If you ask the locals, you'll hear a few different explanations for how the fire started and why the church wasn't able to be saved.

Some say it was a heating oil explosion in the building next door, which at the time was used for maritime storage. Others have more nefarious explanations. They say that as the Cuban Missile Crisis raged on, some of the townsfolk got sick of staring at a Cathedral celebrating Russian culture, and saw to its demise.

Either way, whether you believe the fire was intentional or an accident, the result was still the same. The Cathedral burnt down, leaving both an empty feeling and an empty space in the center of town.

I'm not exaggerating here. At the time, St. Michael's Cathedral quite literally had towered over all of the other buildings in Sitka's downtown. And with it gone, it really did feel like something was missing. So, what did Sitka do? They held a town hall to discuss what to do with the newly unoccupied space. There were a few ideas thrown around but, in the end, it was determined that anything else in that space would look strange. So, the people rallied together to reconstruct the historic landmark.

They used old photographs, original blueprints, and even people's memories to ensure that every board, and every nail, was reconstructed in the exact likeness of the original.

But if you've been to Sitka, or any small Alaskan town, you know that Alaska will always find a way to make things difficult. For instance, sourcing materials that matched the original structure was nearly impossible. Not to mention, Sitka Sound's salty air had faded the church's original blueprints to the point that they were all but unreadable. These obstacles, though, only strengthened the communitiy's resolve and the town's shared beliefs in the importance of restoring this historic building.

And in 1976, just a decade after the fire, the new St. Michael's Cathedral stood completed—its green domes once again dominating Sitka's skyline.

Currently, the Cathedral continues to serve as a place of worship, but it is much more than just a building now, more than just a replica, it is a gathering place where the past and present meet, where the stories of those who built and rebuilt St. Michael's are embedded right in its very walls.

What did the purchase
of Alaska look like?

In the annals of recent history, there are very few events that stand as significant as the Alaska Purchase, a transaction that transferred the vast and rugged expanses of Russian America to the burgeoning United States. But, when it comes to Sitka, this transaction has even more significance because, well, this is where the deal was sealed and the signing of the Treaty of Cession of Alaska occurred—an impactful moment for not just St. Petersburg and Washington, DC, but the world.

We will get to the incident itself soon enough, but some of you, I'm talking about our international readers—and even some of our lower-forty-eight readers—might not have a clue what it is that I am talking about. And for them, it's important that this story starts with a few statistics and background.

Now, if you've already visited Alaska, while you were there you likely walked along Seward Street in Juneau, or you've probably driven down Seward Highway just outside Anchorage, or you've even visited Seward City located on the Kenai Peninsula. Even crazier yet, there is even a Seward Glacier over by Yakutat. But why is everything under the sun in Alaska named Seward?

Well, that is because the terms of the trade were negotiated by none other than US Secretary of State William H.

Seward. Terms which basically said that for the sum of $7.2 million, the United States would acquire what Russia claimed to be theirs in North America. To put this into perspective, that was roughly $0.02 per acre—a heck of a deal for just about anyone.

But despite this outrageously good price, many in Washington didn't believe it was worth it, and the exchange quickly became known as Seward's Folly. And sadly, this is how Seward thought of it when he passed. He did not get the chance to live long enough to see that the purchase of Alaska, the transaction he spearheaded, became one of the most lucrative investments the United States has ever made.

Fun fact, when oil was discovered on the North Slope of Alaska—in other words, the top of the world—the very first truck that made the long journey hauling oil from the Arctic down to the contiguous United States paid for the whole thing. That's right, just one truck made it all worth it. And, if you think about it, that doesn't include all the gold found before, the fish caught along the way, or the fantastic views seen by all of the cruise ship passengers every single summer. Sounds like Seward didn't do too bad after wall.

Anyway, back to the purchase. The deal was finalized in March of 1867. However, to witness the formal transfer of Alaska from Russia to the United States, we need to fast forward to October 18 of the same year. Because on this day, the transfer of sovereignty occurred during a brief yet poignant ceremony atop Castle Hill. Representatives of the two nations stood solemnly on this hallowed ground as Russian soldiers lowered their tricolor banner to the sound of cannon fire—a farewell to an era.

Moments later, the Stars and Stripes

were hoisted aloft, greeted by another cacophony of cannon fire, marking the dawn of American governance in this remote territory. The ceremony on Castle Hill was not just a simple transfer of flags, it symbolized the shifting tides of power, a continuation of the United States' manifest destiny and its strategic foothold in the Pacific.

Now, this transition sounds like a smashing success. There was no battle fought and no blood spilled as one nation took control of a territory and another succeeded it. But, there is one glaring issue with this ceremony—an entire nation was left unrepresented, the Tlingit.

The Russian occupancy of Alaska in its entirety was tenuous at best, based solely on the Doctrine of Discovery and not rooted in the reality of the situation. The Tlingit, along with other Native Alaskans, had long held these lands, with their rights acknowledged in

various ways. One of these was the Peace
Ceremony of 1805 in Sitka—a ceremony
that never once recognized Russian
supremacy or control of the land. This
explains why the Treaty of Cession of
Alaska's language was so vague, leaving
much open to interpretation. Facts which
were swept under the rug in the name of
global diplomacy as two distant powers
determined the fate of a land they barely
understood.

For the Tlingit and other Native
Alaskans, the Cession ceremony was
a bittersweet spectacle. Their lands,
rich with the bounties of nature and
the rhythms of their culture, were now
caught in the crosscurrents of colonial
ambitions. The Treaty of Cession of
Alaska, despite its extravagant promises,
failed to recognize the sovereignty of
the Indigenous inhabitants who had
nurtured and revered these lands long
before European sails appeared on the

horizon. And as they watched from their canoes below Castle Hill, watching as one flag was lowered and another one lifted, a new reality began to sink in—one where their legal status, land rights, and cultural traditions were at risk of being overshadowed by an influx of settlers with a relentless drive for economic gain.

And, as the cannons fell silent and the flags settled into their new positions, the people of Sitka, both Native and newcomer, faced an uncertain future. And, in the end, the story of the Alaska Purchase is not just one of diplomatic triumphs and territorial expansion. It is a story of people, of cultures meeting and clashing, and of promises made and broken. It is a reminder that history is more than just the grand deeds of nations, it is also about the everyday lives of those who experience these sweeping changes. History which, in this case, happened right here in Sitka.

Was Sitka ever really Russian?

So, obviously, today Alaska is owned by the United States. And, in order to attain the state, they paid $7.2 million to Russia. These are facts that are indisputable. However, as we learned in the previous story, Russia's control over Alaska, and over Sitka, was far from stable. The Tlingit resistance was formidable, and the narrative of Russian-Tlingit relations was fraught with conflicts that never found a final resolution. And if that is the case, was Alaska really Russia's to sell?

In the early 19th century, Sitka, Alaska, became a unique intersection of two worlds—where Russian settlers seeking new frontiers met the established Tlingit people whose ancestral ties to the land ran deep. The Russians first arrived in the late 18th century and attempted to establish their presence amidst the Tlingit resistance. Far from a simple tale of conquest, their coexistence unfolded as a complex dance of diplomacy, trade, and uneasy alliances.

To give a little background, the Russians initially tried to secure their foothold in this foreign land through military might, clashing with the Tlingit in a series of confrontations. First in 1802 when the settlers were driven out, and again in 1804 when they returned with a group of ships laden with cannons and forced the Tlingit to retreat. Yet the Tlingit warriors, clad in their impenetrable yellow cedar armor, continued to fight, even if it wasn't from Sitka, but instead a secret sanctuary deep in the forest.

Now, it is essential that I remind the readers here that as I stated before, this retreat was not a surrender. And despite the Russian's advanced weaponry and control over Sitka's ports, the Tlingit's strength and numbers loomed large and they never ceded the land that they'd stewarded since time immemorial— something that the Russian's eventually recognized.

And once recognized, their strategy shifted. Russian authorities began engaging the Tlingit through trade and negotiation, and often observing their laws and customs over Russian ones. One such example of this occurred when a few Russian settlers, eager to exploit Alaska's natural resources, encroached on the Tlingit hunting grounds. To resolve the issue, Tlingit leadership demanded resolution and, rather than entering into conflict, the Russians submitted to the Tlingit council, accepting their verdict and compensating for the transgression.

Another vivid illustration of Russian dependency, not dominance, occurred during a particularly harsh winter. Unprepared for the brutal Alaskan cold, the Russians faced dwindling supplies and starvation. And if the Tlingit hadn't come to their aid, providing food and essential resources, this book might read very differently.

It is the totem poles now that stand as the silent storytellers of this past. A past that witnessed conflict born from ambition, cooperation born from survival, and the enduring spirit of the Tlingit who call this place home. It is with each carving, from the base to the top, that they tell this tale.

That said, unfortunately, the average tourist these days simply looks to these totem poles for their colorful artistry and

is blissfully ignorant of the stories they
tell. The same blissful ignorance shown to
the sovereignty of the Tlingit people and
their rights to the land where Sitka now
resides.

Why is Lord Baranof naked on top of the totem pole?

Sitka is an island town, and the island which it is situated on is called Baranof. And I know what you're all thinking, it sounds Russian. Well, that is because it is.

Baranof Island is named after Alexander Andreyevich Baranov, a rather important figure when the Alaskan coast was occupied by Russia. He has multiple things named after him: the island, buildings and ships, and even statues.

With all that said though, if you've been to Sitka, you've likely walked around downtown and found yourself in Totem Square, a beautiful park near the water at the end of Lincoln Street. And in the center of the Square, there towers a tall pole with a naked man on top. That man, you guessed it, is ol' Alex Baranov himself.

For context, contrary to what some might assume, the tale of a totem pole begins at the bottom and ascends to the top, and the foundational figures at the base are the most significant. They bear the weight of the stories above. Therefore, as the eye travels upward, the carvings become progressively less significant with the top figure being the least important. Meaning, according to the totem pole in Totem Square, in the story of Sitka, Alaska, Alexander Baranov wasn't a key player.

Now, you might be asking yourself, and I wouldn't blame you if you were, why Mr. Baranov finds himself at the top of this totem pole, in the least important position, bearing the brunt of Alaska's unpredictable weather in just his underwear?

Unfortunately, the answer to that question is only somewhat agreed upon. There are a few theories explaining why Baranov is depicted this way, and we'll get to them shortly. But first, you'll need to know a little more about the man himself, so that's where we're going to start.

Alexander Baranov was a tenacious man, born in the far reaches of Russia. And at the time, in order to succeed there, you needed to have ambition, something Alex was chock-full of. This is why, when the position of Chief Manager of the Russian-American Company became available in the untamed wilderness of Alaska, he signed up right away.

While in Alaska, Baranov made a name for himself by expanding the fur trade, forming diplomatic relations with the Indigenous peoples, and winning decisive battles such as the Battle of 1804—

something we discussed in an earlier story. He is even credited for establishing key settlements like Pavlovskaya Gaven and Novo-Arkhangelsk, which are now known as Kodiak and Sitka. But despite all of his successes, the story of Alexander Baranov has a darker side to it.

The Tlingit, who had lived in harmony with the land for generations, found themselves at odds with the Russian newcomers. And Baranov's drive to expand Russia's influence often disregarded Tlingit sovereignty, leading to clashes. Some telling instances were skirmishes, forced relocations, and cultural imposition which left lasting scars on the Indigenous community on both the island and beyond.

Some say it is this less than favorable past that resulted in Baranov's position on the totem pole, acting as a visible commentary of the time when Russians controlled Sitka. And this would make complete sense considering the history between the two groups.

However, this particular pole was commissioned by the U.S. government, and at the time, there were no carvers in Sitka, so it was commissioned to workers in Wrangell. Workers which others say, may have altered the original design.

In the end, regardless of whether it was the initial intent or the influence of other players, Baranov isn't going anywhere any time soon. And, the pole that now bears his likeness is commonly known as the shame pole—a stark reminder of the fact that it doesn't matter how important or influential a person may be, or may have been, there are always two sides to every story.

Are there sunken ships in Sitka Sound?

Up until now we've learned a lot about Sitka, but, what we haven't talked about is the Sound itself. Sitka Sound is a breathtaking stretch of water where the sun shimmers off its surface, reflecting the silhouettes of the towering peaks of Alaska's shoreline. The Sound is also home to a labyrinth of islands, both large and small, multiplying as you draw closer to shore, breaking the open ocean's powerful current and calming the waters into a much gentler, rhythmic sway. However, if you ask one of the locals, you'll find out that this body of water is home to more than one maritime mishap. And, if you're reading this story, I'm guessing you're curious what it is that is out there, lurking just below the surface.

Okay, so yes, the Sound may seem serene while you stand on Sitka's shore, but one must never assume—especially in Alaska. The waters that feed the Sound are from the Pacific Ocean, and out by Mount Edgecumbe there are several currents that meet; there is the Alaska Coastal Current, the Gulf of Alaska Gyre, and, of course, the tidal currents from the Pacific.

And the meeting of these powerful currents creates a nautical nightmare for even the most seasoned seamen. Now, you're not being told this just to be told, it is a key factor in the story ahead—the story of the *Neva*—a prominent ship that

was overwhelmed by the sea's fury, and
met her violent demise at this very spot
... or so I'm told. But first you really need
to hear about this ship's adventures to
understand what made her so important
to Sitka's history. So, let me tell you.

In the early days of imperialist
Russia, the *Neva* successfully
circumnavigated the globe, a feat never
before accomplished by a Russian vessel.
She traveled from St. Petersburg to Cape
Horn and rounded the southernmost
tip of South America. After that, it was
the island life for her crew, traveling to
Easter Island, the Hawaiian Islands, and
eventually the Aleutians. From there,
it was just a short hop, skip, and jump
down the Chinese coast, across the Indian
Ocean, around the southern tip of Africa,
and back to St. Petersburg.

Now, during this trip, the ship spent
little time in Russian-America, but this
success proved the *Neva's* worth and

eventually led to her pivotal role in Russia's operations in Alaska. One such operation being the Battle of 1804, or as it is more commonly known, the Battle of Sitka.

The Battle of Sitka was fought between the Russians and the Tlingit over the area surrounding Sitka. What you didn't learn earlier, though, is that the *Neva* was one of only two ships involved, and the critical naval firepower she provided was instrumental in overrunning the Tlingit stronghold on shore. This event not only cemented the *Neva's* legacy within the Russian Navy, it secured the ship's new port-of-call—Sitka, Alaska.

And that is where she stayed, sailing to and from Sitka transporting supplies, personnel, and furs to Russian settlements along the Pacific coast.

But Sitka was growing in popularity. And, for a time, it was actually the largest colonial settlement on the west coast of the Americas. This improbable jewel of the north had become a hub of Russian culture, boasting grand balls and soirées beneath the glittering chandeliers at the Chief Manager's home. There was even opera.

So, the Tsar decided to erect a cathedral in the center of town. But this wasn't going to be just any old church. No. It was to be a symbol of Russian imperialism. No expense would be spared to adorn St. Michael's Cathedral with treasures from the empire.

And according to the locals, because of the *Neva's* storied history, it was the *Neva* that was charged with the task of travelling to Russia to receive this priceless bounty. Once received, she would then embark on her return voyage laden with valuables destined for Sitka's Russian Orthodox Church.

But as the story goes, the *Neva* would never reach her intended port.

The meeting of the powerful currents near Mount Edgecumbe proved to be too much for the ship, driving her into the rocks and sending her to the depths. And along with her—the precious cargo.

For generations, the tale of the *Neva* has captivated the people of Sitka and treasure hunters the world over, drawing folks from not only Alaska, but around the world. Unfortunately for them, the ship has never been found; her location obscured by the very currents that sealed her fate. But, the legend lives on, brought back to life with every telling of the tales told by those who live in the area. Stories about sacred relics, lost treasure, and the hidden dangers of the Alaskan coast.

With that said, while the ship itself was never found, the sea has occasionally relinquished fragments of her sunken bounty. Among the most celebrated of these is a painting, a sacred icon which washed ashore and now hangs in St.

Michael's Cathedral—a quiet witness to the ship's ill-fated journey.

In recent years, a team of scientists, while surveying nearby Bird Island, uncovered what they believe to be the survivor camp from the *Neva*. Scattered remnants of makeshift shelters and old fire pits hint at the desperate struggle of those who managed to reach the shore. Yet still, despite their meticulous search, no trace of the ship's treasure was found among the ruins.

Thus, the search for the *Neva*—the ship that shaped Sitka into what it is today—continues. Its riches, both lost and found, feeding the curiosities of yet another generation of treasure hunters. And if you are one of the fortune seekers looking to cash in on the *Neva's* lost loot, just remember, stay vigilant, for although the waters may look calm right now, just around the corner there could be clashing currents.

What is the deal
with Bird Island?

If you're reading this story, it's likely you've visited Sitka. And, if while you were there, your travels led you across the choppy waters of Sitka Sound, it might also be true that you puttered past the rugged, windswept isle known as St. Lazaria— affectionately known to the locals as Bird Island. This small, rocky outcrop is a haven for seabirds: gulls, murrelets, auklets, and puffins whom all call this place home, their cries piercing the salty air.

However, there are multiple islands that pop up in Sitka's surrounding waters that don't receive the same kind of attention. And it begs the question, why? Why is this specific island favored by the birds of Sitka? Well, this tale aims to help explain both the scientific reasons and the locals' explanations.

From a scientific perspective, geologists have suggested that St. Lazaria was created through a series of volcanic eruptions where lava flowed slowly, gradually building up the landmass over time. The product of the volcanic ash is the island's rich, fertile soil, creating an ideal environment for plant growth that supports the thriving bird population.

Another scientific explanation considers the unique microclimate of St. Lazaria. The combination of frequent fog, mild temperatures, and abundant food sources in the surrounding waters creates the perfect habitat for seabirds.

Not to mention, the island is more remote when compared to the other options around Sitka—this, paired with its steep cliffs makes St. Lazaria a safe haven from predators and an ideal breeding ground for seabirds.

However, if you ask the locals, they'll tell you a different story about why the birds love St. Lazaria so much. From what I've been told, the origin story of Bird Island begins with Mt. Edgecumbe, the ancient volcano that dominates Sitka's skyline.

As the story goes, long ago, there was an eruption more powerful than any before, which resulted in the very top of Mount Edgecumbe being blown clean off. It soared through the sky, trailing ash and fire, and crashed into the waters of Sitka Sound. And as the newly-formed island cooled, the molten interior continued to flow forming lava tubes underneath its surface. This left behind a network of tunnels and caves beneath the ground, perfect for seabirds to nest and thrive. Yet, this is not the only folklore explaining the island's unique formation and its avian inhabitants.

Another legend speaks of a great spirit bird, the Thunderbird, revered by the Indigenous people of Southeast Alaska. The Thunderbird once roamed the skies, its wings spanning from horizon to horizon. And from what I'm told, one day during a particularly sunny stretch of weather, the Thunderbird became irritated with the lack of clouds. So, in a fit of rage, the Thunderbird struck Mount Edgecumbe with a bolt of lightning so powerful that it split the mountain's peak and sent it tumbling into the sea. The island that formed became a sanctuary for birds, birds which are said to be descendants touched by the Thunderbird's power, forever drawn to their ancestral home.

Now, somewhere in the interplay of these explanations—both mythical and scientific—lies the true essence of St. Lazaria. It is an island that stands defiant against the elements. A place alive with a cacophony of wings and cries that is never truly quiet. And a site where both the natural and supernatural coexist.

When was the last time Edgecumbe erupted?

For thousands of years, Mount Edgecumbe has watched silently over Sitka Sound; the mountain's conical silhouette carved against the Alaskan sky. And for over 4,500 years, this volcano has long been a curiosity for locals and tourists alike—a landmark like none other along the Inside Passage. But when was the last time this titan erupted? The truth is, it depends on who you ask.

When the Russians arrived, Edgecumbe loomed in their journals and sketches, an omnipresent reminder of nature's capacity for creation and destruction. Even during the Gold Rush, as prospectors swarmed the region, it stood still, an ancient monument untouched by the chaos of man.

But by the 1900s, the mountain became less a source of concern and more an object of passive fascination—a postcard backdrop to Sitka's bustling harbor. Truth be told, people forgot about the volcano. That is, until Mount Edgecumbe roared back to life—or so it seemed.

It began on a quiet April morning in 1974, the kind where Sitka Sound mirrors the gray of the overcast and life seems to stand still. Locals went about their routines, and the citizens of Sitka enjoyed predictable serenity. But then, without warning, a plume of black smoke spiraled up from Edgecumbe's crater, twisting ominously upwards.

Within minutes, panic struck the

town. Mount Edgecumbe appeared to be on the verge of eruption. Phones buzzed, residents spilled into the streets, and first responders initiated emergency protocols. Everyone's attention was drawn to the volcano with a mix of awe and terror.

During this time, multiple reports were flooding into the Coast Guard. And as the smoke thickened, forming a dark cloud that cast a shadow over the water, Sitka prepared for the worst.

The Coast Guard scrambled to investigate, dispatching a helicopter to survey the scene. It did one pass, two passes, and eventually, on the third pass, the truth revealed itself—it wasn't magma nor ash, but instead, a smoldering pile of old tires stacked meticulously on top of each other and set ablaze. Next to the fire, carved in giant letters in the snow, was a message: "APRIL FOOLS!"

The mastermind? None other than Oliver "Porky" Bickar, a Sitka local with a penchant for mischief and an impeccable sense of timing. Not only had Porky spent weeks planning the prank, air dropping dozens of tires into the crater by helicopter, he'd also waited three years for the skies to be clear enough for his master piece to ignite the frenzy it did, creating a spectacle that Sitka would never forget.

When the truth spread, fear quickly turned to laughter. The audacity of this—and the sheer scale of his prank—immediately became legend. Even the Coast Guard couldn't help but admire the determination, creativity, and brilliance of the joke, so they let it slide.

As for ol' Porky today, well, he's since passed on, but his memory lives on in the legendary "eruption" of 1974—a piece of Sitka's folklore passed down alongside Edgecumbe's actual geological history. A story that proved that even a dormant giant like Edgecumbe could still spit fire—not from within, but from the boundless imagination of a man who dared to make it smoke.

Why are there
no mosquitoes in Sitka?

If this is your first time in Alaska, you've likely been told about its towering mountains, vast wilderness, and untamed wildlife. But there is always something that typically gets left off of this list—Alaska's unforgiving insects.

Yup, the state is home to a variety of blood-sucking bugs, most notable being the mosquito. There are over thirty-five different species of mosquitoes across the state, some of which grow to be so big that folks say they could very well be the state bird.

That said, Sitka, unlike much of the state, is noticeably free of the buzzing, biting nuisances that plague so many other parts of Alaska. The reason for this curious phenomenon has long been the subject of speculation. And while science offers a clear explanation, the people of Sitka have their own rationales as to why. And if you keep reading this story, you'll get to hear both.

For those less inclined to believe in myths and legends, let's start with the scientific explanations, shall we? And one such explanation is rooted in Sitka's unique climate. The town, nestled between the mountains and the sea, is known for its cool and unpredictable weather, which creates a less than ideal environment for mosquitoes who prefer a warmer, stagnant location.

Another account points to the very

soil beneath Sitka's streets. Sitka Sound and the surrounding region is home to at least seven extinct volcanoes, the most impressive of which being Mount Edgecumbe. Now, Edgecumbe hasn't erupted in several thousand years. However, its most significant eruptions used to blanket volcanic ash all across the area. And over time, this has resulted in Sitka's soil becoming highly acidic and a natural deterrent to mosquitoes.

Both of these scientific theories do a great job of explaining the lack of mosquitoes in Sitka, but to understand Sitka fully, one must look beyond the soil and weather, and into the stories locals share amongst themselves, stories that have been passed down from generation to generation. They offer a far more colorful explanation, one of myth, legend, and folklore.

One such tale speaks of how the Raven, a trickster in Tlingit mythology, saw how the people of Sitka were suffering and took pity on them. And in order to ease the people's burden, the bird flew to the mouth of Mount Edgecumbe and with a mighty flap of his wings, stirred the volcano into a great eruption. The resulting volcanic ash was a gift to the people, acting as a protective barrier against the pests that tormented them.

Another legend tells of a powerful shaman who lived in the shadow of Mount Edgecumbe. And, when the shaman saw the mosquitoes swarm and torment his people, he called upon the spirits of the mountain for aid. Soon after, the mountain roared to life, sending forth a plume of ash filled with the shaman's magic, which rendered the soil hostile to mosquitoes, ensuring the safety and comfort of the people of Sitka.

Regardless of which story you choose to believe though, whether it be based in myth, legend, or science, next time you find yourself in Sitka walking along the waterfront or through the lush, moss-draped forest, take a moment to appreciate the silence. There is no hum of mosquitoes, nor a need to swat or scratch. Instead, all there is, is the wind in the trees, the calls of the birds, and the gentle sound of the ocean lapping against the beach.

And when you actually recognize the peacefulness that is found in so few places in Alaska, you'll realize, it doesn't matter if it was magic, a gift from nature, or a naturally occurring event, you're just happy that you aren't itchy.

Raptors don't still exist, do they?

The answer to this question is quite short. No, raptors in a dinosaur's sense do not still exist. However today, when someone is talking about raptors, they are referring to birds of prey which do still exist. There, done.

The only problem now is, I'm sure there is another question eating at you—the real question that you wanted to ask—what does it take to save a raptor?

In Sitka, the solution starts with one

simple act of compassion: two townsfolk opening their backyard to an injured eagle. And from that modest beginning, the Alaska Raptor Center emerged—a place where the untamed spirit of Alaska's skies meets the healing hands of a community.

The gesture was small, but it ignited a movement, turning one person's backyard into a community-wide effort. And, over time, the small sanctuary has grown to not only save the lives of birds of prey, but also educate, inspire, and connect locals and tourists alike with these amazing animals.

In its beginning, word of the backyard sanctuary spread quickly. Volunteers, moved by the plight of the injured birds, began offering their homes as temporary refuges. Kitchens and living rooms transformed into makeshift aviaries, and the townsfolk's dedication to the cause became the cornerstone of a grassroots movement. It wasn't just about saving birds; it was about a shared responsibility to rescue and rehabilitate the birds of prey in the region.

By 1983, the backyard effort had outgrown its humble origins and moved to a small shed on the campus of Sheldon Jackson College. And it wasn't long until that shed was filled with the sounds of birds in various stages of recovery. Eagles, hawks, owls, and falcons were all soon found within its walls. But the Center's founders were never satisfied, and continued to work tirelessly to provide even more injured raptors a chance at the care they needed to heal and regain their strength.

Thankfully, the community of Sitka, inspired by the work of the Center, rallied behind it, providing resources and support. Even local schools got into the action, incorporating visits to the Center into their curriculum to teach their children about the importance of wildlife conservation.

And eventually, the tourists began to

come. Slowly at first, but eventually they flocked in droves to Sitka, eager at the opportunity to see the raptors up close and personal.

With the increase in visitors came a boost in revenue that allowed the founders to grow their vision. And in 1991, the Alaska Raptor Center moved to its current location, a 17-acre plot of land along the Indian River and across the street from Totem Park—a space that accommodates the treatment of over 200 birds a year, with 25 permanent residents who can no longer fly. This makes it the largest bird treatment center in Alaska.

But, despite all of this growth, the Center's mission remains unchanged: they strive to rescue and rehabilitate injured raptors, educate the public about conservation, and foster a spirit of coexistence between humans and wildlife.

Some of the Center's current projects involve collaborating with other organizations to advocate for policies that would protect raptor populations and reduce human-wildlife conflicts. It has become a voice for the raptors, speaking out on their behalf in the face of growing environmental challenges.

And it's all possible thanks to your support. Today, the Alaska Raptor Center continues to thrive with entire tour buses being shuttled to and from the Center, allowing folks from around the world to see the magic of these majestic birds.

But despite all of this success, the fancy new cages, and the 17-acres of pristine Alaskan wilderness that now houses the raptors, it's important not to forget the center's humble beginnings, the countless hours of care, the unwavering dedication, and the individuals who refused to euthanize the first bald eagle. For the Alaska Raptor Center is more than just a refuge, it is a promise kept to Alaska by Alaskans to protect the Alaskan skies and those who soar within them.

How does one start a bear sanctuary anyway?

That's right, Sitka isn't just home to raptors; it is home to bears, too!

Now, it can't be surprising to the readers of this story that there are bears in Alaska. You don't need to travel this far north to know this. However, what you might not know is that when you visit Sitka, seeing one in close quarters is all but guaranteed. And that is all thanks to the Fortress of the Bear.

Of course, if I only explored the

three-quarter-acre enclosures that offer both aerial and ground-floor viewing opportunities; or I just discussed the survival stories of the bears that eventually called this place home; or I only talked about the amazing people that had the vision that brought this place to life, I'd likely have enough content to fill the pages of this story.

The only problem with this though, is that all three of these factors play a crucial role in making this place a reality. So, to answer your question, how does one start a bear sanctuary? Well, we need to start at the beginning. And that story starts with the Fortress' founders—a couple who shared a love for the outdoors and a love for Alaska.

I must warn you, the beginning of this story is not a happy one. The tale begins in tragedy. Two brown bear cubs were left orphaned after their mother was put down. And for those of you who don't know, bear cubs rely heavily on their mother for a variety of things—food, protection, and critical survival skills—which means that without their mother, the two cubs' odds of survival were very low. So, the wildlife management agency contacted one of the founders—a local hunting guide—and asked them to finish the job. They couldn't bring themselves to do it, and for the next ten years, they worked tirelessly to make sure that this type of a situation never happened again.

The journey wasn't easy. The guide and his partner faced resistance from the town's residents, local government, and environmentalists arguing that it was either unsafe or just flat out wrong to keep wild animals in captivity—even if it was for their own safety! The founders persevered though, driven by the belief that they could offer a better alternative for orphaned bear cubs.

They started by securing a site, a few

abandoned concrete tanks originally built for the former pulp mill in town. That's when the real work began. They needed to design enclosures that mimicked the bears' natural habitat and turn the tanks into a place where bears could not only live safely and regain their strength, but thrive.

They built climbing structures, created water features, and ensured ample space for the bears to explore. Every element was engineered with the bears' needs in mind, creating a space that balanced safety with the need to resemble their natural environment.

And in 2007, their hard work finally paid off in the form of their very first resident, a brown bear cub named Killisnoo. At seven months old and weighing just under 52 pounds, Killisnoo had been rescued by the Alaska Department of Fish and Game in Angoon. This marked a turning point for the Fortress, transforming the once desolate tanks into a place of purpose, a place where Killisnoo had a chance to live a long and happy life.

Since this beautiful bear's arrival, the sanctuary has expanded, welcoming other orphaned and abandoned bears. And with each new bear comes a new story of survival. There was Toby, a playful brown bear who moved to the Fortress after her mother ingested plastic bags and passed away. Chaik, whose calm, quiet demeanor made him a favorite of the Fortress' regulars after his mother wandered into a fishing lodge at 2 am, and the shocked chef defended himself the only way he knew how.

Now, I don't tell you these stories to bring you down. No. They are meant to be reminders of the constant struggle between wildlife and human encroachment, and to shed some light on the importance of places like the Fortress.

More accurately, though, the stories

are a thank you to the Fortress' founders, who prefer to remain anonymous heroes, and those who shared in their vision of coexistence and conservation. I'm talking about the volunteers, the supporters, and those who have donated to this worthy cause. Even the policy makers who originally resisted the idea, but eventually allowed for this important work to move forward. For if it were not for all of these folks, it's likely that these bears, and the many bears to follow, would meet a fate similar to their mothers.

So, as you watch the bears play and listen to them splash in the water, remember what it takes to give these bears a second lease on life, and what is possible when passion meets perseverance.

Author's note

As you come to the end of this book of tall tales, we hope you have enjoyed the wild adventures and colorful characters that have been brought to life through the histories, stories, and folklore that have shaped Alaska and the people who call her home.

But it is important to remember that, although these tales have been shared and passed down by locals over the years, they are not entirely factual. They are the stuff of legend and imagination, embellished with each retelling to become bigger and more outrageous than before.

Nonetheless, these stories have become an integral part of the fabric of Alaska's history and culture, and they continue to inspire and entertain new generations of storytellers and listeners.

So, as you put down this book, remember to take these tales with a grain of salt, and to appreciate them for what they are: a testament to the enduring spirit of the Last Frontier, and to the power of a good story to captivate and delight us all.

Who's your author?

The author telling these tall tales wasn't born and raised in Alaska, but he'll tell you he's from Alaska. He'll tell you that because he's spent the last eight years of his life living in Juneau. But it wasn't the picturesque landscapes that brought him here though. No. Instead, it was an unexpected encounter in the heart of South America that made his life take this remarkable turn.

That's right, he followed a woman all the way up north, past the sixtieth parallel.

However, their initial meeting was bittersweet. Their whirlwind romance in South America only lasted three weeks because she had a job to get back to in Alaska and, at the time, he had a company to run back home. So, they said farewell and went their separate ways.

But, upon getting home, our author knew that something was different.

Something about that girl had left an undeniable mark on his heart. And, driven by this unshakable feeling, he planned a trip to visit her in Juneau.

From the moment he landed in Alaska, he was struck by the towering mountains, lush forests, and the pristine waters reflecting the azure sky above. But, if you ask him now, it was the simple moments spent with the woman he loved that left the deepest impression. Whether it was sharing stories over a crackling fire or embarking on an impromptu hike up Blueberry Hill, every moment felt like a cherished memory.

And with each passing moment they spent together, the author's resolve to build a future with her grew stronger. So, upon returning home, with unwavering determination, he sold his shares in the company and everything else he owned, and embarked on the greatest adventure of his life.

Eight years later, he's now married to the woman he met in South America, and a proud resident of Juneau. A place that has both become his home and the backdrop to his love story—the greatest story he'll ever tell.

So, if you're in Juneau, go ahead and make your way on down to the Red Dog Saloon. And if you're lucky, you might just find him there signing books and passing out pints from behind the bar—or, more likely, drinking them on the other side.